The Crossroads

PRAISE FOR *STORYSHARES*

"One of the brightest innovators and game-changers in the education industry."
– Forbes

"Your success in applying research-validated practices to promote literacy serves as a valuable model for other organizations seeking to create evidence-based literacy programs."

- Library of Congress

"We need powerful social and educational innovation, and Storyshares is breaking new ground. The organization addresses critical problems facing our students and teachers. I am excited about the strategies it brings to the collective work of making sure every student has an equal chance in life."
– Teach For America

"Around the world, this is one of the up-and-coming trailblazers changing the landscape of literacy and education."
- International Literacy Association

"It's the perfect idea. There's really nothing like this. I mean wow, this will be a wonderful experience for young people."   - Andrea Davis Pinkney, Executive Director, Scholastic

"Reading for meaning opens opportunities for a lifetime of learning. Providing emerging readers with engaging texts that are designed to offer both challenges and support for each individual will improve their lives for years to come. Storyshares is a wonderful start."
- David Rose, Co-founder of CAST & UDL

The Crossroads

Grama Jayaram

STORYSHARES

Story Share, Inc.
New York. Boston. Philadelphia

Published in the United States by Story Share, Inc.

Storyshares
Story Share, Inc.
24 N. Bryn Mawr Avenue #340
Bryn Mawr, PA 19010-3304
www.storyshares.org

Inspiring reading with a new kind of book.

Interest Level: Middle School
Grade Level Equivalent: 3.7

9781642615333

Book design by Storyshares

Printed in the United States of America

Storyshares Presents

1

They had to be there by dusk. Otherwise, the whole trip would be a waste.

The sun was already setting. The boy stumbled as he ran, grabbing his servant's arm to steady himself. Both had been running to reach their destination before the sun disappeared behind the hills.

The servant was breathless, but the boy was used to running. He ran everywhere. In fact, he enjoyed this chance to run to the forest.

The boy's mother banned him, as a rule, from playing near the forest. But today was different. Today, his mother *sent* him and the servant into the forest.

2

The boy thought about how worried his mother was about the rash on his leg. For fifteen days, it had resisted her herbal ointments.

She had spoken to all of their neighbors. "Hindu, Muslim, Christian . . . I have exhausted all medical advice," she said.

The "foreign" hospital, which offered Western medicine, was several miles from their village. And it cost too much money.

Then, the milk vendor lady suggested that the boy's rash might need divine help. "For a rash like your boy's, you should make offerings to the forest goddess, Maramma. Just last month, the officer lady in town made an offering. Her son had a rash bigger than the one on your boy's leg. It vanished overnight. Do it today," the woman urged.

The boy's mother asked for details about the offering.

"Two beetle leaves, three beetle nuts, an unbroken coconut, and a five-*paise* coin. Your son must travel to the crossroads at the edge of the forest. He must place them there just as the sun sets behind the hills. Then, he must return home. He can never look back."

His mother took the milk lady's advice. She sent her eight-year-old son, with the servant as his guide, to place the offerings at the crossroads.

3

The boy and his servant reached the forest just as the sun started to slip behind the rocky hills. They stopped to catch their breaths.

The servant held out the bag. The boy removed each sacred item and placed them in the middle of the crossroads.

When he finished, they began walking away. The sun was a flaming sliver on top of the hills. Suddenly, they heard a yell from the trees. In their hurry to complete their task, they had failed to notice the straw huts at the edge of the forest. An old woman emerged from a hut, screaming loudly.

"Hey! Hey, you *sahibs*! What are you doing? Take these away! You will bring us bad luck from the goddess." She pointed at the offerings on the ground. Clearly upset, she came close to the boy and servant, blocking their exit path.

"These offerings . . . take them away. You put them too close to our homes. We do not want the goddess Maramma to visit us."

The boy felt afraid. He looked at the servant, who also seemed scared of the tribal woman's outburst.

Being a mile away from their own village, neither knew how to handle the situation. They did not know who else lived in the huts and feared what might happen if things turned violent.

4

"Where is the man of the house?" the servant asked boldly. "I want to talk to him. You don't understand, woman, who this young *sahib* is. His father is a big officer in town. You don't want to get on his bad side."

The woman smirked. "You are just a boy. I bet you don't even have hair on your face yet . . . Why do you want to speak with a man? I'm good enough. And I'm telling you to get these things out of here now."

The servant tried a new strategy. With a sly look, he lowered his voice and said, "I'll tell you what you can do. As soon as we leave, take these offerings for yourself. A free coconut, beetle leaves, money. What do you say?" He thought he had convinced her with this bribe.

The woman exploded with anger. "Do you think we are foolish? Or crazy? We would not steal from Maramma. I would sooner pet a cobra than steal the coconut offered to Maramma. Ten thousand free coconuts would not convince me to bring down the powerful goddess's wrath."

5

The boy looked at the woman, whose face grew red. He feared she would hit the servant at any moment.

The servant must have noticed the same thing. He switched to pleading. "Please don't misunderstand. I did not mean to insult you. Please let us leave these sacred offerings to Maramma here. When you know what they are for, you will not object. . . . I see you have a young one there."

A young girl, about the same age as the boy, had run up to the woman. She wore a dress with tiny mirrors on it, a smaller version of the old lady's dress.

Her thick black hair was half-braided. It seemed like the woman had been in the middle of oiling and braiding the girl's hair when she saw the strangers and decided to intervene.

The servant continued, "This poor young *sahib* has a rash on his leg. After weeks and weeks, it has not gone away, even though they have tried all types of medicines. They even tried taking him to the foreign hospital."

Although the servant lied, he felt it was for the boy's own good. "Sir, why don't you show your rash to this good mother?" he asked the boy.

6

"Does it hurt a lot?" asked a small voice.

The young girl had moved closer to look at the rash.

"A little bit, sometimes." The boy felt proud to have something to show. After all, not every boy had a red rash. "But I don't care. I play a lot, rash or no rash."

"Really?" The girl smiled. "What games do you play?"

The boy rarely spoke to girls since boys and girls went to different schools and played separately. This moment was a special occasion.

If other boys were around, he would not have spoken to a girl. But now he was interested. Besides, she seemed to admire him. "I play many games: Gilli Danda, catch a thief, soccer," he said.

"I play in the forest. The other day, I found a beautiful stick. Do you want to see it?" she asked.

He hesitated. This was new to him. He did not know the rules of talking to a girl. He seemed to like it. Also, he loved sticks. He had dreamed of running to the forest, cutting down a branch, and making a bow and arrow with beautiful sticks. He decided to accept the girl's offer.

7

While the boy and girl spoke, the woman bent down to look at his leg. After feeling the rash with her fingers, she made up her mind.

As they all entered the hut, the girl picked up two sticks from a corner. The old woman lifted a large folded leaf from a hanging pot. A green paste filled the inside of the leaf.

"Please, show me the rash again," she said to the boy. With warm water from a pot on the stove, she cleaned the rash. Then, she rubbed a large handful of the green paste onto it. Afterwards, she wrapped the leaf around his leg.

"There. You will be cured in three days. This is very good medicine." She turned to the servant. "Please tell his mother there is no need to be afraid. Tell her the goddess gives gifts in strange ways. When they come to us, we may not always recognize them."

The servant seemed unimpressed. He did not want to oppose the woman, but he was not sure if the boy's mother would approve of this herbal medicine.

8

The servant looked at the boy, who was admiring the sticks. The girl explained how to make the sticks smooth. She swung a stick in the air to show how it swished and sang.

Wanting to show his superior knowledge, the boy said, "We can pretend they are swords."

They both swung a stick back and forth, dangerously close to the adults.

The servant decided to accept the old woman's medicine.

When the boy and the servant began to run home, it was dark. The boy held a stick, a gift from his new friend. He had agreed to look for more sticks in the forest with her, if his mother let him.

The boy and the servant ran fast past the crossroads. As they sped by, they both noticed that the offerings were gone.

About The Author

Jayaram is 77. He was born in India and has lived in America for 50 years. He earned a Ph.D. from UCLA, spending 32 years in the corporate world as the chairman of two firms and a consultant to many.

Since 2004, he has run two non-profits; one in India and one in the U.S. to serve the education of underprivileged children. His organization, Institute of Leadership & Institutional Development (ILID), runs five schools for 1,400 children in two Indian cities. ILID delivered online tutoring to 1,250 underprivileged students in 25 schools in New York, Washington DC, Philadelphia, and southern California.

In 2014, he published a volume of poetry and a book on leadership called, *How to Help an Elephant Make a U-turn?* His play, *The Costume Party*, has been performed to sold-out theaters and standing ovations.

His complete portfolio includes three plays, 25 short stories, a memoir, and a volume of poetry. Works-in-progress consist of a novel called *The Twice Born* and three plays.

He won awards at the Philadelphia Writers conference for his poems and a non-fiction piece. He won the best story award at the Moth Story Slam in New York.

He wants to write beautiful works. He hopes to enhance the quantum of joy in the universe.

About The Publisher

Story Shares is a nonprofit focused on supporting the millions of teens and adults who struggle with reading by creating a new shelf in the library specifically for them. The ever-growing collection features content that is compelling and culturally relevant for teens and adults, yet still readable at a range of lower reading levels.

Story Shares generates content by engaging deeply with writers, bringing together a community to create this new kind of book. With more intriguing and approachable stories to choose from, the teens and adults who have fallen behind are improving their skills and beginning to discover the joy of reading. For more information, visit storyshares.org.

Easy to Read. Hard to Put Down.

www.ingramcontent.com/pod-product-compliance
Lightning Source LLC
Chambersburg PA
CBHW071231170626
46809CB00005BA/2031